HAILEY PUBLIC LIBRARY
7 WEST CROY ST.
HAILEY, IDAHO 83333
(208) 788-2036

T *Is for* TERRIBLE

PETER McCARTY

SQUARE
FISH

HENRY HOLT

I am Tyrannosaurus Rex.
I am a dinosaur,
otherwise known as
a terrible lizard.

I do not know why
I am so terrible.

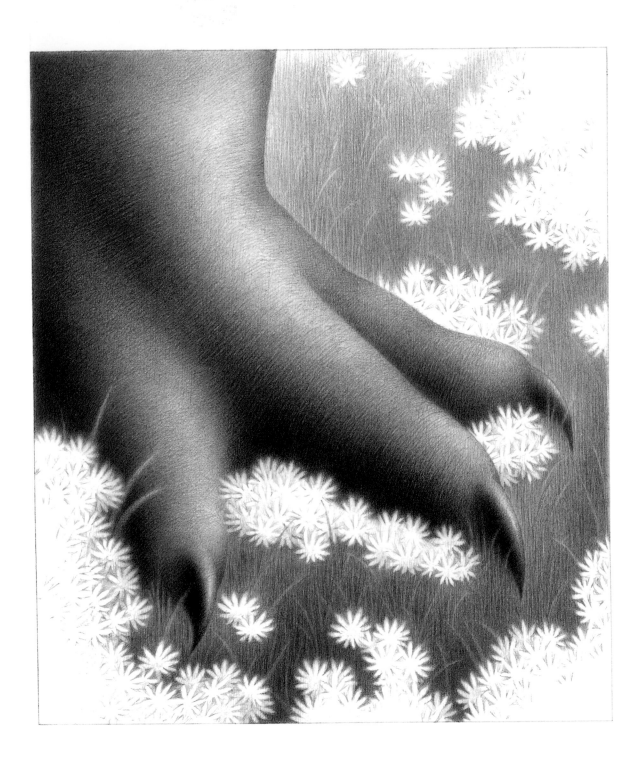

I cannot help that I step
on little flowers when I walk.

Or that the
ground shakes
when I run.

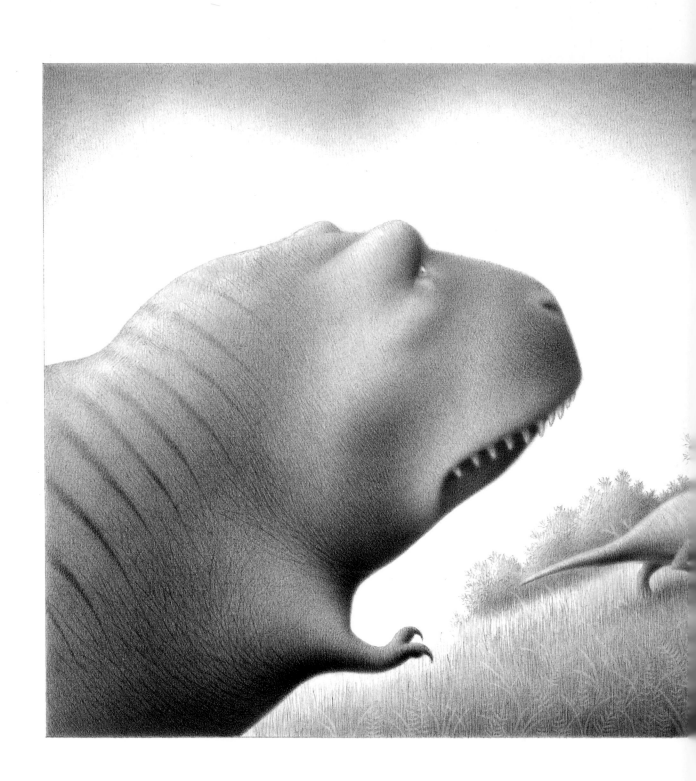

Would I be so terrible
if I were pink?

Or blue?

I am much like
other creatures.

When I was born,
I came out of an egg.

I too had a mother.

As I became older,
I grew and grew.

I cannot help
that I grew so
enormous and
so enormously
hungry.

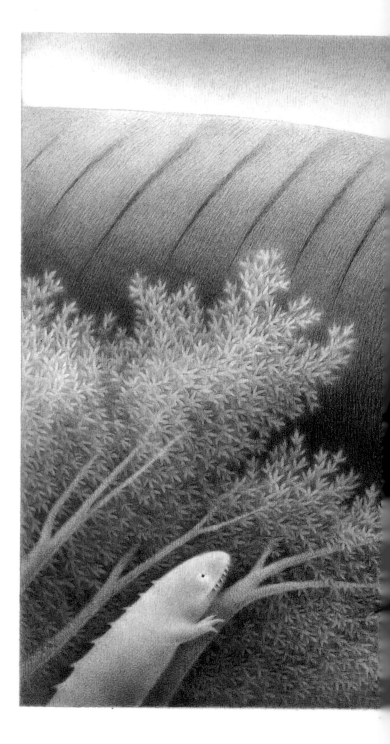

If I could,
I would be a vegetarian.

But I am Tyrannosaurus Rex,
and I do not eat trees.

I cannot help that
I am so terrible.

TO HENRY

SQUARE
FISH

An Imprint of Macmillan

T IS FOR TERRIBLE. Copyright © 2004 by Peter McCarty. All rights reserved.
Printed in China. For information, address
Square Fish, 175 Fifth Avenue, New York, N.Y. 10010.

Square Fish and the Square Fish logo are trademarks of Macmillan
and are used by Henry Holt and Company under license from Macmillan.

Library of Congress Cataloging-in-Publication Data
McCarty, Peter.
T is for terrible / written and illustrated by Peter McCarty.
Summary: A tyrannosaurus rex explains that he cannot help it
that he is enormous and hungry and is not a vegetarian.
[1. Tyrannosaurus rex—Fiction. 2. Dinosaurs—Fiction.] I. Title.
PZ7.M12835 Tae   [E]—dc22   2003018246

ISBN-13: 978-0-312-38423-4 / ISBN-10: 0-312-38423-8

Originally published in the United States by Henry Holt and Company
Square Fish logo designed by Filomena Tuosto
The artist used pencil on watercolor paper
to create the illustrations for this book.
Designed by Donna Mark
First Square Fish Edition: September 2008
10 9 8 7 6 5 4 3 2 1
WWW.SQUAREFISHBOOKS.COM